A Midnight Symphony

Maria M. Rodriguez

A Midnight Symphony
Copyright © 2022 by María M. Rodríguez

Art by
María M. Rodríguez

ISBN:
9798218113582 - Book
9798218113605 - Epub

Library of Congress Control Number:
2022922943

I dedicate this book to my mother,
Luz María Rodríguez, who was
courageous, compassionate, generous, kind,
and full of joy.

TABLE OF CONTENTS

Contents

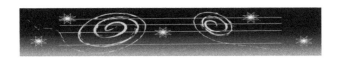

At the Beach

The beach was Araceli's favorite place.
She swam, built sandcastles, and searched
for seashells there. She loved their shapes,
their colors, their texture, and even the way
they smelled of salt and ocean. One day
she found the biggest seashell ever. Most
days she left the seashells at the beach.
This one was special. Etched on the inside
was a hieroglyphic of what looked like a
snail. Araceli carefully placed the seashell
in her beach bag and took it home.

That evening, before going to bed,
Araceli cleaned the shell then placed it
over her ear. To her surprise, she did not
hear the usual sound of the ocean, or
any sound. *Okay, she thought, there is
something stuck in the shell.* She took a
deep breath, placed her lips to the shell,

and blew as hard as she could. Nada. Too tired to try again, Araceli placed the shell on her nightstand and went to bed. As she drifted into sleep, she dreamt that she was at the top of a mist-covered mountain.

She's the One

While Araceli slept, a dog carrying a coquí frog and a small parrot on his back, walked up to Araceli's bedroom window.

"This is the place," screeched the parrot excitedly. "This is where the little girl with the magic seashell lives. She's the one who can call the animals."

"Shhh," said the dog. "You might wake her."

The coquí saw that the window was partly opened. "I will wait inside," he said as he hopped into the room and climbed into the seashell. The dog and the parrot yawned widely. "I'm going to catch a few winks," squawked the parrot.

The dog, sounding irritated, snarled as quietly as he could at the parrot. "You can't help being loud, can you?"

The parrot perched in the nearest tree branch, and in his most quiet voice said, "see you in the morning."

The night was calm and cool. The dog and the parrot slept soundly.

A Tiny Echo

As the sun came up, the rooster crowed loudly, "It's morning! It's morning! Everyone get up!" He continued crowing until Araceli stirred.

Her first thought was about the seashell. Gently she picked it up from the nightstand. She grinned. This was the rarest shell she had ever found. Slowly, she traced the outline of the snail etching. "Let's see if the ocean is in this shell today," she said, as she pressed the shell to her right ear.

Nada.

"Maybe there's something wrong with this ear," she worried, as she switched the shell from her right ear to her left ear. This time a tiny echo reverberated from inside the shell.

"Buenos días, señorita. I am Paquito."

Araceli threw the shell onto her bed. A

coquí frog peered from within the seashell. Araceli's big brown eyes met Paquito's amber-colored eyes. She opened her mouth as if to say something, but like the seashell, no sound came out.

Paquito came a bit closer. "I am delighted to meet you."

Araceli continued to stare at the tiny frog, which by then had hopped to the windowsill. She knew coquíes could sing. She had never heard one speak.

Words started to form in her mind.

Slowly she managed to softly say her name. "Araceli. I am Araceli."

Another surprise waited for her on the other side of her bedroom window. There she saw a medium-sized yellow dog. On its head was a Puerto Rican parrot, an iguaca. She could tell by the red band above its beak.

Araceli gasped. She did not know what was more surprising, a talking coquí, or an iguaca. Catching a glimpse of an iguaca was a miracle. They were almost extinct.

Araceli took in a deep breath. *"So, okay," she told herself. "This is what happens in dreams."*

Gently, she placed her palm out inviting Paquito to hop on. Like most coquíes, Paquito was less than an inch in size.

"I have an important message for you," Paquito announced. "Let's go outside so you can properly meet my friends."

Still thinking she was dreaming, and knowing all things were possible in dreams, Araceli stepped outside.

The iguaca wasted no time introducing himself. "I am Enrique, el numero uno," he squawked as he puffed his feathered chest. "Most enchanted to meet you!"

The dog lifted an eyebrow, looking at Enrique disapprovingly.

"I am Bartolo," he said in a deep but easy voice. "Just Bartolo."

7

Araceli suddenly felt at ease. Paquito was polite. Bartolo had an easy-going manner. Enrique was quite beautiful, even if a bit loud.

"I am Araceli," she repeated, then, looking straight at Bartolo, she smiled tenderly and added, "just Araceli."

Enrique cleared his throat, "Ahem!"

"Paquito's abuelo, Don Gregorio, is worried that there will come a time when the song of the coquí will no longer echo throughout the island. What would this island be without the coquí's song?" he asked.

Araceli listened as Paquito hopped from her palm to the porch banister.

"It's the noise," added Paquito. "There is so much noise from machines. Rat-tat-tat. The streets are full of cars: honking, beeping, and screeching. How can the coquíes song be heard through all that racket?"

"And at night," added Bartolo," there are too many lights. I can barely sleep."

"They keep knocking down trees and clearing land."

Enrique paced nervously. "One of these days there might not be one tree standing for me to perch or nest in," he added, shaking his head sadly.

Araceli knew that Enrique was in worse danger. She learned at school that the Puerto Rican parrot was in danger of becoming extinct. Other animals around the world were in danger of disappearing too.

"I just don't know how I can help," Araceli said somberly.

Paquito studied her. "My grandfather said we had to find the girl with the magic seashell."

"That's you," squawked Enrique. "Bartolo saw you at the beach the other day. You picked up the magic seashell and took it home."

9

"It is unusual," Araceli said. "But magic? I don't know how. I blew as hard as I could into that seashell. I could not hear a whisper of a sound come out of it."

Bartolo nodded. "Paquito's abuelo said that the magic seashell will only make a sound when you blow into it from the top of a mountain peak."

Araceli remembered her dream the night before. She had been standing on a mist-covered mountain peak.

"What will happen when I blow into the seashell at the tower?" Araceli shifted uneasily.

Paquito regarded her: "Animals that are in danger of disappearing will hear the call!"

"Don Gregorio, Paquito's abuelo, said that once they arrive, they will play a beautiful symphony, which will be heard around the world," Enrique went on.

"Maybe then," said Paquito, "the people

will stop to listen and decide to help."

"Do you mean the animals here on the island," asked Araceli?

"No. No. All animals in danger of extinction around the world," Paquito responded.

"But…" Bartolo wrinkled his brows. "Some birds might be able to fly here. Some water animals can even swim here. But how do you suppose polar bears or monkeys would get here? What about elephants, lions, or tigers?" he asked.

Araceli nodded thoughtfully. "They would have to travel long distances. It could take weeks, or months for them to arrive," she said. "I don't know how that's going to be possible."

For a moment, everyone was silent. It felt as though a balloon had burst, and all the air was leaking out.

Paquito closed his eyes. He took a deep breath. Then another. "Those are

good questions," he said calmly. "My
abuelo didn't tell me how that was going
to happen."

Enrique soared skyward, then fluttered
like a falling leaf to a nearby tree branch. "I
say we go forward," he squawked loudly.

"Go forward how, where? We can't
just get up and go," insisted Bartolo, who
paced slowly from a nearby tree to the
windowsill, and back to the tree again. We
need a plan."

Plan? Araceli wasn't even sure this
conversation was real. She wasn't ready
to move an inch forward. What she really
wanted was to awaken from this vivid
dream where parrots, dogs, and coquíes
talked!

The Invitation

Paquito crashed Araceli's thoughts. He jumped onto Araceli's shoulder and yelled in the loudest voice that a half-inch frog could muster: "Look. Look what's coming," he said as he pointed his tiny digits toward a nearby Tabonuco tree.

At first, everyone looked up at the sky. But what was coming, was on the ground.

Araceli gasped as she took a step closer to her front door. There she saw an iguana the size of a canoe. It was bright green, like a lime. In its mouth was an orange envelope covered with penny-sized white polka dots.

"How odd?" said Bartolo. "What do you suppose an iguana wants with us?"

Paquito, Enrique, Bartolo, and Araceli stared. Their jaws dropped as an exceptionally large iguana waddled toward them. They all gasped as the iguana stopped inches away. Silently, the iguana dropped the envelope at Bartolo's feet. Then, before any of them could fully breathe again, the iguana simply faded away.

As soon as he felt safe, Enrique swooped down, and picked up the envelope with his beak.

He hovered around Araceli's head, insisting she open the envelope.

"Here," he said. "I never learned to read."

Araceli giggled. She knew parrots could imitate sounds, but she'd never heard of one who could read.

"Thank you, Enrique," she said, as she took the envelope and sat on the porch stairs.

Everyone watched and waited.

Araceli, unhurriedly, read the invitation: *You are all invited to a night of music at the El Toro Peak in the El Yunque National*

Forest, tomorrow at midnight. Please wear your spiffiest clothes and bring your favorite musical instruments. P.S. It is important that Araceli first blow the seashell at the Yokahú Tower in El Yunque before noon tomorrow. Failure to do so means not one endangered animal will know to show up at El Toro Peak. We look forward to seeing you all tomorrow at midnight.

Small Beads of Sweat

Araceli had barely put the invitation back into the envelope when Enrique squawked, "A party! Oh my. Oh, my. I love parties! I'm already dressed in my spiffiest clothes! Don't you just love my green and turquoise feathers? How about the beautiful red band above my beak?"

"I don't know if I can stay up that late," complained Bartolo. "I don't own a musical instrument. I can't even play a musical instrument." Then, in a hopeful tone, Bartolo asked "Do you think my yellow coat is spiffy enough?"

"I think it is most lovely," Paquito chimed in. "And I wouldn't worry about not having a musical instrument. Look at me. I don't play an instrument. Still, all over the island the people love my singing."

"I have heard you howl rather loudly my friend," added Enrique. "You just need to tame it up a bit. Your voice can be your instrument. Then Enrique reassured Bartolo about his looks. "A good brushing will give your fur coat a brand-new look."

Bartolo fixed his droopy eyes on Araceli, who suddenly covered her ears with her hands, and raced into her house. Araceli's mind had focused on the last part of the invitation: *Failure to do so means not one endangered animal will know to show up at El Toro Peak.*

"Oh dear," Bartolo sighed. "Maybe things are happening too fast."

"She needs time to think," Paquito whispered.

Enrique flapped his wings and perched on the highest branch nearby. "I'd leave her alone for awhile!"

Once inside her room, Araceli's bed creaked as she threw herself onto the mattress, face first. She pulled her pillow over her head. All kinds of thoughts boomeranged inside her brain. *Was that really an iguana? What instrument could she play? Could she wear her favorite jeans? And the Yokahú Tower? It was 75 feet tall!* Araceli remembered that tomorrow her class was taking a trip there. *It was a trip that she had been dreading all week. And didn't she read somewhere that El Toro Peak was over 3,000 feet above sea level?* That last thought made Araceli's heart sound like the beat of conga drums.

Small beads of sweat formed on her forehead. She knew she had to slow down. She closed her eyes tightly. *Breathe in. Breathe out. Breathe in. Breathe out.* She learned to do that at her mom's yoga class.

After a few minutes, her head felt cool. Slowly, her breathing steadied.

She glanced at the seashell laying on the nightstand. She picked it up. With all her heart she hoped that when she pressed it against her ear, she would hear the ocean.

Nope. Still nada.

Araceli sighed deeply. Holding the seashell, she walked over to the window. Bartolo lay slumped on the porch. Enrique paced atop Bartolo's head. Paquito pensively sat on the porch banister.

Uneasily, Araceli stepped out onto the porch.

Bartolo quickly rose, forcing Enrique onto the banister, where he widely stretched his wings.

Paquito hopped hesitantly toward Araceli. They all looked at her expectantly.

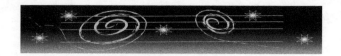

Alarma de Caracol

"What if we just return the seashell to the sea?" Araceli finally spoke. "Maybe I'm not the one who was supposed to find it."

Bartolo howled anxiously.

Enrique flew to higher ground.

Paquito sadly stared at Araceli, his amber-colored eyes now looking gray. This was not what he was hoping to hear.

He inhaled deeply. "Let me tell you a story," he said softly. Listen carefully."

Araceli sat down on the porch. Hands clasped on crossed knees, she listened intently.

"A long time ago," Paquito began, "before you or me or Bartolo or Enrique were born, even before your mother, my grandfather and his grandfather, a *really* long time ago, the Taino people lived on this island. They lived peacefully with plenty to eat, beautiful views of the mountains and the sea, and safe shelter. One day, the cacique, also known as the chief, looked out to sea. He saw large ships with big sails headed to the island. Having never seen a ship like that, he was both curious and worried. What was that contraption? What or who did it carry? Would it be good news for his people, or danger like the stormy huracanes? The cacique selected a group of his bravest warriors to ride out into the ocean to investigate. As they got closer to the ship, they saw men with hairy faces. They had something shiny on their heads. Araceli knew about the Tainos and about the Spaniards who came to the island from across the sea. It must have been very scary to see bearded men with metal helmets on their heads. She also knew that huracanes were hurricanes. However, she did not interrupt Paquito.

"The warriors, frightened by the sight

of the men on the large ships, decided to go back to land. Before furiously paddling back to land, one of the warriors stood tall in the canoe. He pulled up a large seashell. In those days blowing into a seashell was a warning, like an alarm system. They called it the *Alarma de Caracol*. The brave warrior had to warn his people about the potential danger as soon as possible. As the warrior stood to blow the seashell, a large wave crashed against the canoe. He lost his balance and almost fell into the ocean. Lucky for him the other warriors held onto him, but the seashell fell into the sea. Down into the sea it quickly sank. Without the seashell, the warriors were not able to give advanced warning to their tribe about the mysterious ship and the dangers it might bring.

Bartolo and Enrique, fascinated by Paquito's story, wanted to know what happened next. Araceli had other things in mind.

In her most patient voice, she asked, "Are you saying that the seashell that fell into the sea ages ago is the same seashell that I found?"

Before Paquito could respond, Araceli, now sounding more suspicious, added, "There are thousands, probably millions of seashells in the sea and at the beach."

Paquito responded with a question. "How many seashells have you seen or found at the beach that had anything etched inside of them, and specifically, a snail?"

Araceli stood. Arms crossed, she stared at Paquito without saying a word. She knew Paquito's response was not a clear answer, but he had a point: there was that snail hieroglyphic etching on her seashell that she could not ignore.

Araceli took a deep breath. It did not matter whether the seashell she had found was the same one as the one the Taino warrior had dropped into the sea centuries ago. Araceli had to tell them the truth.

High Up

"I...I'm afraid of heights," she said, staring down at her feet. "El Toro Peak and the Yokahú Tower are way up high in the mountains."

Enrique dove straight from his perch onto the porch.

"I live up in the forest canopy, a few thousand feet from the ground where you are standing," he squawked. "I often have aerial battles with the dreaded guaraguao, the fierce red hawk. And when I was just a chick, even I was afraid of heights. With practice, practice, practice, I don't even think about it now. I just do it," he said confidently.

"You're a bird," Araceli scolded Enrique. "You have wings. You can fly!"

"I can't say I'm afraid of heights," says Paquito calmly. "We coquíes live all over the island, not just in the mountains. We even hang out on the coast."

"Well, just so you know, Araceli, I absolutely, to the limit, understand. I don't like heights either," Bartolo nodded. "I try to stay in coastal towns myself. The higher you go up into the forest the less light there is. It can be slippery and rocky too. Rocks are hard on the toes. No. I'd rather just stay by the coast."

Araceli walked slowly over to where Bartolo flopped. She stared into his big brown eyes. She could tell that he was feeling anxious.

"It so happens," she said, as she petted Bartolo gently," that tomorrow our science class is taking a school bus trip to El Yunque. Then staring again into Bartolo's eyes, she said, "I don't…ah…I didn't want to go, but," she said trying to sound as upbeat as possible, "I've changed my mind! I'll blow into the seashell from the top of the Yokahú Tower."

Enrique got so excited he nearly squawked himself into a sore throat.

Paquito hopped around the wooden banister repeatedly saying, "sí, sí, sí!"

Bartolo began to whine nervously.

Paquito, and Enrique ignored Bartolo and offered to go with Araceli to El Yunque.

"I'll fly along, overhead, "Enrique declared.

"I could hide inside the seashell," Paquito proposed.

In all the excitement, even Araceli seemed to have forgotten about Bartolo's anxiety. "I would really love the company," Araceli beamed. "Still, it would be better if you just ride along inside my backpack. I don't want to forget that you are in the seashell. If a loud sound does come out of the seashell, your little ears might burst!"

Enrique squawked loudly. "That would be a hoot."

"Not so very funny," Paquito sneered.

Bartolo interrupted the mood with a pitiful howl.

All eyes fell on him.

"If you don't mind, I will just wait here," he said. "El Yunque is too far, and too steep," he added.

Enrique asked Bartolo to think about it differently. "It's not *that* far. You walked to the beach with us. You walked here. El Yunque is around the corner! You can do it, Bartolo!"

"That might be true," Paquito said. "But it's like a thousand feet or more above sea level. That's a steep climb for anybody."

"Anyway," Bartolo argued, "I don't believe they allow my kind there."

"Actually…" Araceli corrected Bartolo. "I have seen people walking the trails of El Yunque with their dogs. They just ask that dogs be on a leash."

Bartolo held his head high as he said

with determination, "There will be no leash around this neck. Nope. I will just wait here."

To make sure that this was the last word, Bartolo flopped heavily to the ground.

Surprisingly, he wasn't there for long.

The Chauffeur

A gurgling sound erupted from within the seashell, followed by a steady stream of bubbles, like those made with a bubble maker wand.

Bartolo leapt to his feet.

Enrique did what he did best: he hightailed his feathered body to the highest tree branch he could find.

Cautiously but curiously, Paquito, hopped closer to the seashell.

"Be careful," Araceli warned, as she herself took a couple of steps back.

When the gurgling sound and the surge of bubbles stopped, something small and slimy pulled itself to the edge of the seashell.

"It's a snail," blurted Bartolo.

Araceli stared at the snail remembering the snail shaped hieroglyphic. It was quite beautiful with a pinkish yellow spiral-shaped shell, and long eye lashes.

"My friends," the snail eloquently began. "I am here to let you know that I will be the chauffeur who will take you to El Toro Peak."

Enrique snickered from his branch. "Now I have heard everything."

Even Bartolo chuckled. "Ha. You gotta be kidding."

Paquito hopped even closer to the seashell. Here was a creature with which he could almost meet eye-to-eye. Still, he was so awestruck he could not even say 'boo'.

"I know. I know. You cannot imagine that a tiny creature, such as myself, can be a chauffeur. I won't try to explain. You will just have to believe. Please meet me here tomorrow night at 10 p.m. *on the dot*," he emphasized.

Having said that, the snail disappeared into the seashell almost just as quickly as it had arrived, minus the gurgling and bubbly pomp and circumstance.

"No wonder I can't blow into that seashell," said a startled Araceli. "A snail lives in it!"

"If that's true," exclaimed Enrique "you might not be able to blow into the seashell tomorrow from the Yokahú Tower."

"That can't be true," insisted Paquito. "My grandfather is absolutely sure that Araceli will be able to blow into the seashell."

"That might be so, but I don't see how that creature can take us to El Toro Peak," said a bothered Bartolo as he trudged slowly away from the group. "I think I have had enough excitement for one day. A shaded palm tree at the beach is calling to me."

"You'll be back, right?" Paquito pressed as Bartolo lumbered away."

Bartolo just kept on walking without responding.

Araceli sighed deeply. "It's going to

be a long day tomorrow," she said as she quickly left the porch and went inside.

Paquito hopped off to see his grandfather. He wanted to keep his abuelo up to date on the goings-on of the day.

Enrique, not put off by anyone's mood, flew off squawking loudly, "Tomorrow is going to be a day of great adventure!"

Ninety-Eight Steps

The following day Araceli awakened as usual to the sound of the rooster crowing: *It's a new day. It's a new day. Everybody rise and shine!*

She gazed quickly at her nightstand. The seashell was still there. *This is for real she thought.* "Today will be like no other day in my life," she whispered. Today she had agreed to be la *Alarma de Caracol.*

But Araceli did not feel like a brave Taina warrior. She was feeling scared. Just thinking about climbing the 98 steps to reach the top of the Yokahú Tower made her stomach and her head feel woozy. She had been to the top of the tower once when relatives came to visit. Not wanting to embarrass her mom by making a big stink, Araceli took many deep breaths and managed to climb each step of the tower to the top.

Just as Araceli stepped into her
slippers, her mom stepped into her room.

"I left a bowl of oatmeal on the
table," she said, as she landed a quick
kiss on Araceli's forehead. "I also left a
little something in case you want to buy
something at El Yunque." As she left for
work, she added, "Don't be late for the
bus, corazón."

Araceli grinned. She loved when her
mother called her corazón. It meant their
hearts beat as one.

While she was sorting through her
clothes, she remembered what the
invitation had said. Please wear your
spiffiest clothes.

Araceli picked her favorite shorts. They
had a red and yellow rose stitched on the
pants pockets. She was about to select
a T-shirt when she heard a tap-tap-tap
on the window. She could see that it was
Enrique.

"I'll be out in a minute," she yelled, as

she put on a canary yellow T-shirt.

Enrique and Paquito waited patiently. They both wondered if Bartolo was going to show up.

As Araceli stepped out to wait for the school bus, she noticed that Bartolo wasn't with them.

"Where's Bartolo?"

"I didn't see him after he left yesterday," Paquito frowned.

"I have no idea where he is," Enrique also frowned. "I do know he is having gigantic doubts," he continued. "If I were to guess I'd say he is afraid of heights, just like you, Araceli. "He might not be coming with us."

"He will come," Araceli said firmly. "Still, I don't blame him for being afraid. Everyone is a bit afraid of something sometime—but excuse me," she said, suddenly changing the topic. "There's the school bus! I have to go!"

Enrique flew upward. "I'll follow along," he squawked.

"Forgive me," Paquito added. "I know I told you I'd ride along in your backpack to the Yokahú Tower but right now it's more important that I find Bartolo. I want him to be with us this evening for our trip to El Toro Peak."

As Araceli gathered her backpack and headed to the bus, she yelled out, "It's okay, Paquito. I can't imagine going to El Toro Peak without Bartolo!"

The Yokahú Tower

Araceli walked to the center of the bus where she sat on an aisle seat. As usual she placed her books on the window seat next to her, a window seat she usually set aside for Gloria, her best friend. But on this day Araceli wished she didn't have to save a seat for Gloria.

Gloria always asked a thousand questions. She wanted to know everything about everything. Worse than that, Gloria would want to tag along wherever Araceli went. How would she be able to go to the top of the tower without Gloria following her? Any other day, Araceli would have loved Gloria's company. They could even hold hands as they climbed the stairs together to the top of the Yokahú Tower.

Araceli kept her eye on the front door of the bus. No sign of Gloria. Araceli waited and worried.

She did not feel comfortable telling anyone about the seashell, not even Gloria. *Would the seashell even make one sound if Gloria came, or anyone else? Did the invitation say she could bring a guest?*

She didn't have to tell Gloria the whole story, Araceli told herself. She could show Gloria the seashell, and tell her how she found it at the beach. Then she'd explain that she just wanted to hear the seashell sound echoing through the forest.

Araceli felt better. Maybe there was nothing to worry about after all.

As she glanced to the front of the bus, she saw Alberto, the best speller in her class. Behind him was Andrea, Gloria's cousin, followed by their teacher Ms. Martinez. Gloria was nowhere in sight as the bus driver closed the door and warned everyone to stay in their seats once the bus started moving.

Once Araceli realized that Gloria was

not going to be on the bus, she removed
her books from the window seat. Alberto
decided to sit there. "Sorry," he mumbled
as he almost tripped over her feet.
Araceli smiled shyly and said, "It's okay."
Andrea rolled her eyes and shrugged
her shoulders as she walked by. She took
the last empty seat behind Araceli. Ms.
Martinez took a seat at the front of the bus.

As the bus pulled away from the
parking area, Andrea tapped Araceli's
shoulder. "Gloria told me to tell you
that she wasn't coming today," Andrea
whispered. "She has an upset stomach.
Her mom said she probably ate something
that didn't agree with her."

"I hope she gets better soon," Araceli
tried not to sound relieved.

Amid the noisy bus chatter, Araceli's
mind circled back to the seashell and the
tower. How would she be able to blow
into the seashell without her classmates

seeing her? Could she sneak away for one small moment? How? Would she get into trouble if she snuck away?

The bus drove uphill on a steep incline. Araceli cringed as they zigzagged higher and higher on the mountain curves and past the Visitor Center at El Yunque. She tried not to show her anxiety while Alberto was sitting next to her, but she felt every curve right in the pit of her stomach. Araceli heard her own heartbeat, again beating like conga drums. Instead of enjoying the scenery of lush vegetation, waterfalls, and blossoming flowers of every kind and color, she focused on her doubts. I should not have listened to Paquito, Enrique, and Bartolo she thought. If she managed to find herself at the top of the tower alone, would the seashell make the smallest of sounds? Her doubts screamed: *You can't do it! You are going to fail! You will let everyone down!*

Before she could calm her mind, the bus arrived at El Yunque rainforest. It was too late. She couldn't turn back now.

The bus stopped at the Yokahú Tower parking lot. Once there, Araceli's excited classmates, including Andrea, quickly exited the bus and raced to see who would be first to arrive at the top of the tower. Araceli did not join the race.

She glanced upwards. The tan colored tower was broad at the bottom and got narrower at the top. Observation windows were stationed at three levels. Araceli took a deep breath. She knew El Yunque was a sacred place for the Taino people, the first humans to inhabit the island. The spirit of Yokahú, the supreme deity of the Taino people, in the guise of misty white and bluish clouds, surrounded the tower and filled the forest. Araceli inhaled deeply. Shaky, but knowing what she must do, Araceli took the first of 98 steps to the top of the tower.

Her feet felt as if they were weighed down by giant boulders. Stiffly, she climbed the spiral staircase to the first of the tower's observation windows. She stopped briefly to admire the lush greenery.

She met no one going up or going down. Nevertheless, she knew her classmates, who were already at the top of the tower, would soon be on their way down. As she climbed to the next level, the passageway along the spiraling staircase became narrower. Hazy shadows fell on its walls. Araceli inhaled slowly, trying to calm the nerves that made her legs feel rubbery. By the time she had reached the third level, she was panting. She stopped briefly to catch her breath. She heard the murmur of voices above. She also heard a hushed squawk," Psst. Psst."

It couldn't be Araceli thought. She edged closer to the window ledge. Flying in place, his wings stretched widely, was Enrique!

"Enrique," Araceli's voice echoed excitedly from the tower's walls. "You came!"

"I'm just passing by," Enrique winked. "Just a few more steps and you're at the top! You can do this."

Stomp. Stomp. Stomp.

A stampede of human feet shook Araceli's brief sense of relief.

Enrique hastily flew off.

Araceli stood flat against the tower walls as her classmates noisily headed down the stairs past her.

A boy she recognized as Carlos, yelled out, "Turtle poke, turtle poke."

"It's starting to rain," warned Andrea, as she too ran past Araceli.

Araceli could not let the rain stop her. She had to blow into the seashell. She had to do it before her teacher found out that she was missing. She had to do it before noon.

At the top of the tower a group of tourists wearing shear rain ponchos, lingered.

Would they stay long? Was it close to noon?

Araceli didn't wait to find out.

Clumsily, she dug into her backpack.

By the time she pulled the seashell out, she was glad to see the tourist moving out.

With little time to spare, Araceli selected a spot from which to blow the seashell. As light rain fell on her face, she took a deep breath before briskly blowing into the seashell again and again.

Wonnnnnnnk! Wonk. Wonk. Wonk. Wonk. Wooooonnnnnnnk! Wonk. Wonk.

The sound of the seashell echoed loudly throughout the forest.

At first, Araceli squealed happily. "It worked!

Then she wondered? Had *she blown*

45

the seashell in time? What was supposed to happen? For how long should she blow?

Heavy footsteps interrupted her thoughts. Clumsily she shoved the seashell into her backpack. And just in time. A new group of tourists, also wearing ponchos and carrying umbrellas, surrounded Araceli.

Had they heard the loud sound of the seashell? Araceli did not stop to ask.

"Excuse me, excuse me," she blurted as she struggled to get past them. She had to catch up with her classmates. She was excited to return home to catch up with Enrique and Paquito, and hopefully, with Bartolo too. Had they heard the seashell?

As Araceli ran to the bus trying to outrun the rain, Araceli's teacher met her with an umbrella and a stern look. Silently, a drenched Araceli walked down the aisle to take her seat. She noticed that the window seat was empty. Alberto was now sitting in the back of the bus, talking with another classmate.

Andrea looked at Araceli and smirked. Araceli shrugged her shoulders and slithered into the window seat that was now empty. As she tried her best to dry up a bit, the squeaky bus pulled out. Araceli searched outside the window, looking for Enrique. She was sure he was still around, somewhere.

Before long she caught a glimpse of him. In a spunky move, Enrique glided outside her window. He hovered there long enough for Araceli, and a few alert classmates, to get a quick look-see as he flashed out of sight.

"Look, look," they shouted. "An iguaca is following the bus!"

Some of her classmates jumped from their seats to get a better look, but just as quickly, Ms. Martinez scolded them to get back to their seats.

It was just as well. Enrique had jetted off and camouflaged into the forest canopy.

Araceli beamed. She took in a deep calming breath. For the first time ever, she enjoyed the view and the curves of the mountains as the bus zigzagged its' way down to her coastal town.

From Stone to Stone

While Araceli was on her way to El
Yunque, Paquito hopped as fast as his little
frog legs could carry him, straight to the
beach. Everything Bartolo needed was at
the beach. First, there were the palm trees.
The large fronds supplied shade from
the vibrant sun, and a bit of shelter when
it rained. Bartolo could also find people
at the beach. Where there were people,
there was food, a lot of food. Before
shuttering his food kiosk, one vendor, put
out two old and banged up pie tins for
Bartolo. One was full of leftover rice and
beans. Several times during the week, the
vendor threw in leftover pieces of chicken,
naturally, without the bones. The other tin
was filled with clean water. Yet, it wasn't as
simple as that for Bartolo to fill his belly.
Most days Bartolo had to wait until late in
the day to eat. And if Bartolo wasn't quick

enough, or if he didn't know what time the tins were left, he had to growl menacingly at stray cats who were also hungry and waiting for those tins.

For Bartolo, getting to the beach also meant crossing a busy road, which in the early mornings and late afternoons, were full of anxious, angry, distracted and tired people all trying to get here and there as fast as possible.

Fortunately for Paquito, he didn't have to cross *that* road to find Bartolo. He discovered a longer but safer route, through wooded areas that allowed him to hop from leaf to leaf, from stone to stone, from branch to branch. That path led Paquito right to Bartolo's favorite snoozing palm tree. That's where Paquito found Bartolo loudly snoring.

"Psst. Psst," Paquito whispered as close to Bartolo's ear as he could reach.

Bartolo stirred for an instant, but then

went on snoring.

Paquito hopped right below Bartolo's nostrils. Unable to tolerate the hot air Bartolo was breathing in and out, he hopped onto Bartolo's snout. Once there, he hopped up and down hoping to get Bartolo's attention.

Bartolo opened one eye. Catching sight of Paquito, he opened the other eye and yawned.

"You need to get up. You had us all worried when you didn't show up this morning," Paquito scolded Bartolo.

Bartolo didn't mean to be rude, and if he could have stopped the loud yawn that escaped from him, he would have. He shook himself awake, and with a light whine, he lumbered to all fours.

"I'm quite hungry," he muttered.

"Of course, you are," Paquito agreed. "It is already past noon. We need to get back to Araceli's place!"

"The snail said to be ready by 10 p.m., *that's tonight*," Bartolo flatly grumbled. "Besides that, I *still* don't know how a small snail is going to chauffeur us to El Toro Peak. I *still* don't know how animals living on the other side of the world, will arrive. I *still* don't know how to play an instrument. I *still* don't have anything spiffy to wear and," he hesitated, "El Toro Peak hasn't shrunk. It is *still* sky-scraping steep. You know I hate being that high up, Paquito. I feel dizzy thinking about it." Having said all that, Bartolo plopped down as if he were going back to sleep.

"No. No. Get up," Paquito pleaded. "I don't have answers either, but I trust my abuelo. Besides, you waited right there with us, outside Araceli's window. You were even upset when you thought Araceli would not agree to take on this mission. You're just having cold paws," Paquito insisted.

Bartolo grudgingly pulled himself up.

"How about you take a dip in the ocean, that'd wake you up and clean your coat at the same time," continued Paquito in his most cheerful voice.

Bartolo paced.

Paquito silently waited.

"A bath in the sea is exactly what I need," Bartolo finally spoke. "I'll tell you what, Paquito. "I'll meet you at Araceli's later this evening, when I've had something to eat."

"I can wait for you to take your bath. Araceli can get you something to eat at her house," Paquito pressed. "We can go back together."

"If you're worried that I won't show up," said Bartolo as he ambled to the seashore, "don't be. I heard the Alarma de Caracol. I heard the wonk."

Quite the Star

When the bus screeched and whined to a halt, Araceli grabbed her backpack, waved goodbye to her teacher and friends, and ran home to her porch, where Enrique and Paquito were waiting. She noticed that Bartolo was still missing.

"Hi," she said uneasily.

"If you are worried about Bartolo, don't be," said Paquito confidently. "He'll be here later this evening. We heard the call, Araceli, all of us did. "We are so proud of you."

"You did?" Araceli squealed. "You heard it all the way here?"

Enrique nodded happily. "We did. Loud and clear: *Wooooooonnnk!*"

"I couldn't have done it without your help," Araceli said as she smiled at Enrique. "I felt unsteady climbing up those 98 steps. But just when I thought I could not take one more step, there you were, like a little angel with wings."

"You didn't let your fear of heights stop you! Flying to the top of towers comes easy for me," replied Enrique.

Araceli felt closer than ever to Enrique. She knew that iguacas were one of the most endangered birds in the world. They only lived in Puerto Rico. In her science class, she learned that once there had been millions of iguacas all over the island. Over the centuries, they were hunted for food, killed off as pests, and sold as pets. Hurricanes took a big toll on their population. The clearing of the land and forests left them with few places to call home. Unable to build nests or find food, they almost disappeared completely. There were only hundreds left in the wild and in aviaries.

"No, Enrique," Araceli said solemnly, "You are the one who is brave. You are the one who has fought to survive!"

She turned to Paquito. "The kids on the bus went wild when they saw him. He was quite the star!"

"That's me," Enrique squawked proudly. "Beautiful, beautiful me." He spread his wings to show off his turquoise inner feathers.

"And you Enrique, and your survival, are one of the main reasons we are going to El Toro Peak," Paquito reminded everyone. "Now, what's our next move? Remember, we must meet up here by 10 p.m."

"I have some chores and homework to do," she told them. "And then there's my mom. I hope she goes to sleep early as usual, so I can slip away for a bit." Then, to ease her sense of guilt about sneaking away to El Toro Peak, Araceli added," My mom loves iguacas, and coquíes. I think she'll understand."

Paquito stretched and yawned. Hearing the word sleep reminded him that he hadn't taken a nap all day, what with chasing after Bartolo.

"As you know, Araceli", he yawned drowsily, "us coquíes start singing at sunset. Abuelo will expect me to join him. "Oh, dear," Paquito fussed. "It's going to be a long night. I better get started."

"I need some palm fruit," Enrique said, remembering that he'd been flying light. "But I'd better watch out for the guaraguao. He might make a feast of me!"

"What do you mean," Araceli said with alarm.

"I'm sure you know about the dreaded guaraguao," Enrique said, his eyes wide.

"The red-tail hawk," Araceli gasped.

"The very one," exclaimed Enrique. "They hunt us mercilessly."

"I've seen you do some fancy aerial maneuvers," Paquito reminded Enrique.

"Maybe you can just hang around here," suggested Araceli. "I'm sure we have some fruit in the house that you'd like."

"I didn't mean to alarm you," said Enrique regretfully. "I should have kept my thoughts to myself. He squawked as he flew off zigzagging this way and that, showing off his aerial talents.

You Have One Minute

After eating her supper, doing her chores, and tackling her homework, Araceli plopped down onto her bed. She wondered how she'd leave the house without her mom knowing about it. *What if her mom woke up and did not find her in her bed? She still did not believe that a tiny snail could carry them all to El Toro Peak, and by midnight. How? How? How?*

Araceli soon drifted into sleep. She did not hear her mother's footsteps as she walked into her room and gently placed a blanket over her. She did not feel the kiss on her forehead, or her mom's voice saying, "Buenas noches, corazón."

Araceli dreamt that she was looking up into a starry sky. Among the millions of stars, she saw hundreds of hot air balloons, large, medium, and small, all covered in dazzling and colorful designs. Each carried a different animal. There were armadillos, baboons, chimpanzees, wild dogs, elephants, ferrets, gorillas, polar bears, and so many more. The hot air balloons floated above her house.

Araceli stirred. In the back of her mind, she heard a 'tap,' tap,' tap.' She tried to ignore the sound, but the tapping seemed to get louder. Araceli slowly and sleepily opened her eyes. Then she heard a 'psst.' She glanced at her clock. It was almost 10 p.m. "Oh my," she blurted out as she realized that the tapping sound was coming from her bedroom window.

"Bartolo," she softly whispered as she saw Bartolo's face plastered flat on her windowsill.

Quietly she opened the window. Before she could say anything else, Bartolo whispered, "The snail has arrived, and you won't believe what you are going to see!"

Araceli stepped out into the night.

In front of her was the snail. But it wasn't slimy and tiny. This snail was gigantic and had become a talking hot air balloon!

"Come. Come," said the snail excitedly. "Our friends from around the world are arriving and waiting for us."

Araceli felt unsteady. She didn't feel so good either.

Bartolo saw Araceli's ashen face and suddenly he didn't feel well either. He began to pant.

"Now, now," said Enrique, "there isn't time for neither of you to be afraid. The snail here seems to be an excellent chauffeur. Besides, it looks like a lot of fun." With that Enrique flew into the hot air balloon.

Paquito tried to inspire Araceli and Bartolo. "Give it a shot. We have gotten this far, and it is almost 10 p.m."

"What happens if we don't get on by 10 p.m.," Bartolo asked, stalling for more time.

"If your four paws and her two legs are not in the basket precisely by 10 p.m.," warned the snail, "I disappear, and you will have to figure out how to get to El Toro Peak by midnight all on your own," the snail said bluntly. "Now. You have one more minute to get unscared."

Araceli took a deep breath and quickly moved to climb into the hot air balloon. She extended a shaky hand to Bartolo and said, "Come Bartolo, we have each other."

And so it was that exactly, by 10 p.m., Araceli, Bartolo, Enrique and Paquito, were floating high above Araceli's home, and into the starry night sky.

No one said a word until they were high above the treetops and El Toro Peak was within sight. Araceli pointed to a magnificent scene below and yelled out, "Look!"

On top of El Toro Peak was a stage with many seats. Bartolo stood on his hind legs, holding tightly to the edge of the basket. "I must be dreaming," he said nervously. Then he added, "How much longer are we going to be floating up here?"

"We will be landing in a few minutes," the snail interrupted. "Please hold on, and do not ask any more questions. All is well." From that moment, the hot air balloon made a quick downward descend.

Araceli and Bartolo, and even Enrique and Paquito, closed their eyes and held on as if suddenly they would crash. Had they opened their eyes they might have been more scared. With every inch downward, the hot air balloon shrank in size.

By the time they had all landed on El Toro Peak, and before Araceli, Bartolo, Enrique and Paquito could think about jumping out of the basket, they found themselves standing on solid ground. Mesmerized, they watched as the snail, now back to its original size, exclaimed,

"We have arrived. "Now if you will excuse me," he said as he held on to a rather large tuba, "I have to find my seat."

Maestro!

Shortly, hot air balloons were landing everywhere on the mountaintop. Animals of every species, carrying a variety of musical instruments, climbed out from hot air balloons. Parade-like, they headed to a large stage where each took a seat. Once seated, the animals picked up their musical instruments and stood silently waiting for the conductor.

Araceli almost laughed aloud when she saw a tall ostrich grab a blue kazoo. A small monkey seated to the right of the ostrich, pulled up a wooden flute. Araceli gasped when she saw an elephant almost sit on top of the small monkey. The small monkey chattered wildly, startling the elephant to quickly find another seat. The elephant carried a large drum hanging from his neck.

The sight of a large tiger making his

way to the stage sent Enrique squawking loudly to a nearby tree. Bartolo quickly hid behind the same tree. Paquito jumped on top of Araceli's head at the sight of a mountain gorilla, which took its seat at a piano.

Araceli froze with delight.

"There is no need for anyone to worry," a small voice said firmly. It was Don Gregorio, Paquito's abuelo.

"Abuelo," screamed Paquito. "How happy we are to see you!" Bartolo and Enrique nodded in agreement.

"We are ready to begin," said Don Gregorio. "Each of you must find a seat. Hurry!"

As Araceli walked to find a seat, the old coquí stopped her. "No. Not you. You are to be the conductor. You will lead our midnight symphony. Here is your baton."

Araceli protested at once. "No, no. I can't," she cried. "I have never done this before. I don't know how."

"If you can find a magic seashell, blow it from the Yokahú Tower, and then arrive at the top of El Toro in a hot air balloon piloted by a small snail, you can do this," the old coquí assured her.

Araceli was not convinced. She closed her eyes hoping that upon opening them, she would find herself in the comfort of her home, tucked into her warm blanket with her mom sleeping in the other room.

"Look over there, "Don Gregorio continued as he pointed to the stage, "You have the support of your friends, Enrique, Paquito, and Bartolo." Look at them. They are ready and waiting for us."

Araceli opened her eyes. Enrique was ready with a pair of maracas. Bartolo was picking on guitar strings.

"Where is Paquito?" she asked the old coquí. "I don't see him."

"He has taken his seat in the chorus section," Don Gregorio said calmly.

Araceli searched the stage. At the front of the stage, she saw hundreds of tiny chairs, a coquí sitting in each one of the chairs waiting quietly. One of them was jumping up and down. Although she could not be sure, she figured it had to be Paquito trying to get her attention.

"Araceli, look at me," said the old coquí firmly but kindly. "Everyone has the music within them. I will be on the music stand right in front of you. Just do with your hands and your baton what you see me do."

Araceli faced the orchestra. There were hundreds of chairs, each seating an animal that was in endanger of extinction. All of them had some sort of instrument. All of them looked to her, waiting for her direction.

Araceli trudged to the center of the stage. She felt all eyes on her: yellow tiger eyes, brown gorilla eyes, green coyote eyes, orange eyes of owls, blue cat eyes, eyes of sloth and crocodile eyes—eyes of every shape. Araceli focused on those that belonged to Bartolo. She saw them as soft and reassuring.

Araceli took a deep breath. "I am ready."

"First, please pick up the seashell and blow into it," said Don Gregorio. "We will need to get everyone's complete attention."

Araceli promptly blew into the seashell.

Wonk! Wonk! Woooooonk! Wonk! Wonk!

At the sound of the seashell, everybody on stage picked up their instruments. They stood at attention, all eyes on Araceli.

What Araceli did not know was that when she blew into the seashell, the cue was not just for the animals to begin playing. The sound from the seashell would to be heard around the world.

Those who were sleeping would hear the call in their dreams. Those who were working would suddenly looked up from their desks. Those who were playing at the beach, acting on stage, kicking a ball at the park or on a field, those eating tacos and those eating sushi, and even those in hospitals and in the middle of a war zone, would all stop when they'd heard the seashell—when they heard the *Alarma de Caracol.*

"Now stretch your arms wide, like this," instructed Don Gregorio, as he extended his limbs wide.

Araceli did exactly what Don Gregorio asked her to do. In an instant, all the animals played their instrument. The group of coquíes in the chorus section began to sing:

Listen. Listen.

From forest, mountains, valleys, and plains—

From canyons, deserts, seas, and all terrains—
We've gathered today to sing a song to you.

Listen. Listen.

We sing to the stars.
We sing to the trees.
We sing to the wind.
We sing to the stones.
We sing to every blade of grass.
We dearly sing to you.

Do you smile when you hear the coquí sing? "Coquí. Coquí."
How do you feel when the gray wolf howls yearningly into the moonlight?
Does the siren of the humpback whale make you wonder?
Does the nightingale's song bring cheer to your heart?

*Are you awe-struck when a polar bear
stands up straight?*

*Does the power and beauty of the
Siberian tiger knock you out?*

We shout. We shout.

Listen. Listen.

We have gathered today.

*There might not be for us a glistening
tomorrow.*

We are endangered.

Listen. Listen.

The Alarma de Caracol has echoed.

The iguaca has squawked:

Iguac! Iguac! Iguac!

Did you hear it?

Did you hear it?

Listen. Listen, closely.

We sing to the stars.
We sing to the trees.
We sing to the wind.
We sing to the stones.
We sing to every blade of grass.
We dearly sing to you.

See us.
Hear us.
Save us.

We are one.
We are one.

Bravo!

After everybody had played the last note and sung the last lyric, the total silence that followed, baffled Araceli.

She turned toward Don Gregorio. "I don't understand. Usually, at most concerts, there is an audience. Here at the top of El Toro Peak everyone is on stage. There is no audience to applaud. There are no cheering fans. No one is roaring, "More! More!"

Don Gregorio hopped onto Araceli's palm.

"Look around, Araceli," he urged.

Araceli saw that all eyes were fixed on her, even those of Bartolo, Enrique, and Paquito.

"You see," said Don Gregorio, "You, Araceli, have been the audience. Everyone here has played and sang for you! And with good reason. When you befriended

Bartolo, Enrique, and Paquito, you understood that working with others is important to make a job easier. When you blew into the seashell from the Yokahú Tower you showed us you cared more than you were scared. When you blew the seashell this evening, you showed us that you were ready to act. *We* applaud *you*!"

At that moment everyone on stage stood up and shouted, "Bravo!"

Don Gregorio, who had hopped back to the music stand, bowed as he faced Araceli.

Araceli felt as light as a leaf carried by a gentle breeze. She felt as though at any moment she would float high up into a sky full of blinking stars.

"It is a beautiful night," said Don Gregorio as he gently hopped onto Araceli's shoulder. He then pointed to the chorus section.

Araceli saw coquíes gathering around a

grand piano. The mountain gorilla seated on the piano stool invited them to hop onto the piano keys.

Plunk! Tink! Dum!

Each time a coquí jumped on a key, a new sound filled the air. A 9-foot gray ostrich opened its beak and loudly boomed. A grizzly bear, standing tall on flat feet, joyously beat on conga drums! The rest of the coquíes grabbed a partner and began to dance.

"Hop on," Araceli said eagerly as she put out her palm for Don Gregorio and headed to where the coquíes hopped merrily.

On the way to join the dancing coquíes, Araceli wondered what would happen next? Don Gregorio had sent Paquito, Enrique, and Bartolo to find her. She had found and blown into the magic seashell. Was a call from the seashell and a song at El Toro Peak enough to save endangered animals?

"Every step no matter how small, helps," said Don Gregorio.

Araceli gasped. Had Don Gregorio read her mind?

"Once you make up your mind to help," he continued, "you can find ways to make things better. Now, may I have the first dance?"

The thought of dancing with Don Gregorio transformed the worried frown on Araceli's face to a beaming grin. "I think you would have more fun dancing with someone your own size," she said as she bent down to let Don Gregorio step off her palm.

"I completely understand," replied Don Gregorio as he joined the hundreds of coquíes who were twirling and swinging with their partners on the dance floor.

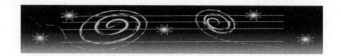

Small Steps

Meanwhile, Enrique was sitting atop a giant fern on the lookout for Araceli, Paquito, and Bartolo. With his keen vision he first spotted Araceli. In one swoop he was by her side.

A startled Araceli simply cried out, "Enrique!"

"I told you this was going to be a blast! Listen to the conga drums. What do you think of the tambourines? And the horns, they are a hoot! But what I really want is to eat," he said as he raced to a table filled with delicious food. The sight of fruit, nuts, seeds, and even cheese, cakes and ice cream made Enrique forget all about finding Bartolo or Paquito.

But Araceli had not forgotten. She spun slowly around searching in all directions. When she finally stopped, she came face-to-face with an emperor penguin.

"Goodness," Araceli cried out. "You startled me."

"Excuse me, Miss," said the penguin in his most polite tone. "Would you like to waltz with me?"

Araceli stared at the penguin, at first not sure of what to say or do.

"I…ah…ah, don't know how to…waltz, but I…ah…ah can follow your steps," she stammered, as she extended a hand to the penguin.

The emperor penguin laughed and took her hand. "I am the only one around here that is allowed to have cold feet," he joked.

Araceli grinned and just like that, she found herself dancing a waltz with an emperor penguin in the midst of a large crowd of elephants, rhinos, orangutans, leatherback turtles, pandas, hippos, iguanas, brown bears and polar bears, arctic foxes, whooping cranes, tigers, leopards, jaguars, gorillas, spotted owls, condors, woodpeckers, and bumble bees along with hundreds of coquíes and other animals from around the world.

"I heard the sound of the seashell all the way in Antarctica," said the emperor penguin as he stepped forward with his left foot, then stepped sideways with his right. "When someone says your kind might be extinct in a couple of decades you pay attention," he continued, as he stepped back with his right foot, moving Araceli along. "Thank you for caring, being brave, and bringing us all together here this marvelous evening," he added.

Araceli did her best to follow the penguin's lead. She wanted to tell him that she really wasn't all that sure if blowing into the seashell was going to be enough. She wanted to tell him that she wasn't even sure that most people, the ones who could make the most difference, had heard the *Alarma de Caracol*, or, that if they did, would take any steps to help the animals. But Araceli did not say any of those things.

"Every step no matter how small, helps, and once you make up your mind to help, you find ways," is what Araceli finally said as she concentrated hard on not stumbling or stepping on the emperor penguin's feet.

She was concentrating so hard that she did not notice that Enrique, Paquito, and Bartolo were watching on the sidelines as Araceli and the emperor penguin danced in step. That is until Bartolo let out a whooping howl that caused both Araceli and the emperor penguin to trip over each other's feet.

"Whooooeee," he said, in the most cow-boyish accent he could muster.

"Did you have to yell like that?" Araceli scolded Bartolo. "I was just starting to figure out the dance steps." Then facing

the emperor penguin, she said, "I am
so sorry. This is Bartolo, and the coquí
and parrot on his head are Paquito, and
Enrique."

"It's okay," said the emperor penguin as
he bowed to them all. He turned to Araceli.
"It was lovely dancing with you. Now I must
be off. It is time to get back home." He
bowed politely and waddled away.

"Did he say it was time to leave," a
bewildered Bartolo asked.

"I think he said *he* had to leave," said
Enrique. "He didn't say anything about *us*
leaving. Let's get some more food!"

Bartolo stretched. Paquito struggled
to keep his eyes opened. Araceli yawned
widely.

"How do you suppose we will get back
home?" Araceli asked as she yawned again.

"Look," Paquito said as he pointed to the
sky.

Hot air balloons floated up to a

sapphire-colored sky. Many were already filled with passengers waving goodbye to one another. Araceli recognized the emperor penguin in one of them and waved.

"Bummer," scowled Enrique, as Araceli asked, "Where's our ride back?"

"Ah hum," said a familiar voice. "No need to worry. Here I am, right on time." The little snail pointed to his tiny watch. "But you must hurry. I want to get home too!"

Araceli and Bartolo eagerly climbed aboard, forgetting their fear of heights, Paquito, and Enrique, who suddenly also felt tired, joined them.

Once all of them were on board the snail said, "Please close your eyes."

Araceli wanted to ask why but she was too sleepy to utter a single word. Wearily, she did as the snail asked. She closed her eyes tightly. Soon the stars, her friends and El Toro Peak itself, faded away like rising mist.

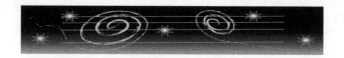

A Catchy Tune

When she opened her eyes again, Araceli was staring at her bedroom ceiling.

"How? Where? What happened," she whispered to herself. "Enrique, Bartolo, Paquito?"

She bolted out of bed. Her gaze fell on the nightstand. The seashell was still there.

Then she noticed that she was still wearing the same clothing she had worn to El Toro Peak.

The last thing she remembered was closing her eyes and feeling sluggish. *I must have slept all the way through the ride back*, she thought to herself.

Araceli walked over to the window in her room.

She noticed the early pinkish-yellow light of sunrise filtering through the curtains.

As she drew the curtains and opened

the window, she expected to find Bartolo, Enrique, and Paquito resting peacefully on her porch.

But they weren't there.

Araceli took a deep breath. The morning air, cool and fresh, filled her lungs. It washed away a sadness that was trying to take a hold of her.

She took in another deep breath and started walking away from her window. But just as quickly, she stopped, enchanted by a series of familiar sounds.

First, she heard the faint song of a coquí: "Coquí. Coquí. Coquí."

Then she heard the squawk of an iguaca: *"Iguac! Iguac! Iguac!"*

Her heartbeat quickened.

A dog barked in the distance.

"Paquito! Enrique! Bartolo!" She thought.

Araceli stood still, listening intently.

She half expected to see Bartolo

lumbering down the road to her house. She searched the trees above. She thought she saw the fluttering of a bird. Enrique? All around her the song of the coquí was quieting.

The sound of her mom's voice pulled Araceli's attention back into her room.

"Corazón, what are you doing up so early? And why are you still wearing yesterday's clothes?"

Araceli stared down at her clothes. She wasn't ready to tell her mom about the gathering at El Toro Peak. She might never be.

"I was thinking that we could go to the beach this morning," Araceli tried to change the subject. Her mom looked skeptical. Araceli tried again. "Ah, uh, "they're still clean."

"It wasn't in my mind to go to the beach, corazón, but why not? It looks like it's going to be a turquoise-color sky day!

But first," she insisted, "you need to wash up and put on some clean clothes. Then come into the kitchen. I will fix us some sweet plantain tostones. Don't be long, corazón," she added.

Araceli could hardly wait to get to the beach. But once again she thought about Paquito, Enrique, and Bartolo. *Would she ever see them again? Where had the snail dropped them off?*

As she packed her beach bag, she saw the seashell on her nightstand. She noticed how beautiful it was with its alabaster white interior and its pearly pink interior. She picked it up and slowly traced the snail shape etching. Nervously, she held it up to her right ear. "Wow!" she cried. "I can hear it. I can hear the ocean!"

She paused and lowered the shell for a small moment. What sound would it make if she blew into it now? Araceli raised the seashell to her lips. She hesitated. *What if the seashell sounded like it did at the top of El Toro? What would her mother think?* Luckily, she would not have to do any explaining. Just then her mother called out to her impatiently.

"Araceli, if you want to get to the beach before it gets too hot you need to hurry."

Quickly, Araceli tossed the seashell into her beach bag.

In the kitchen her mom was standing over the stove frying the tostones and humming a tune. Araceli listened. *Could it be*, she wondered?

"Mom," Araceli called. "What is that song you are humming?"

Her mom placed a plateful of tostones and eggs on the kitchen table. "I'm not sure," she said sounding as surprised as Araceli. "Last night I dreamt that I was at a concert. The band was playing a song with a catchy tune. I don't remember the words to the song, but the tune has stayed with me." She laughed and went on, "And there was this loud wonk sound too."

Araceli smiled. If her mom had heard the song, and the sound of the seashell, everyone around the world must have heard them too!

"Do you remember any of the words?" Araceli pressed.

"I can't think of them now, but who knows. Perhaps later, when I am not in a hurry. Now, let's go. I want to get a shady spot at the beach. Under a palm tree would be nice."

Fly-By Poop

Araceli and her mom found the perfect spot. They found plenty of large palm trees to sit under since there were few people at the beach so early in the morning. Most of the people now at the beach were out for a morning stroll or a jog. Araceli and her mom planted their beach chairs, small cooler, and their blankets and towels under a large and shady palm tree.

"I want to jump in the water," Araceli said, heading toward the seashore.

"Not so fast," said her mom. "Let's get you some sunscreen."

As her mother began lathering her back with gobs of lotion, Araceli looked up at the sky, searching for any sign of Enrique. If he were at the beach, he'd be up high, and camouflaged within the palm fronds. Araceli knew that Enrique, like most iguacas, preferred to be at high altitudes within the forest canopy. But Enrique was bold. He just might fly to the beach.

Just then Araceli felt something land on her hair. At first, she thought her mom had accidentally squeezed sun lotion in the wrong direction. But when she heard a loud squawk and caught a glimpse of turquoise feathers flying high above her, she realized this was *not* lotion. It was fly-by poop!

"Uck!" she screeched.

Araceli's mom tried to squash a giggle.

"You know what we say on the island," she said laughing. "When a bird poops on you, it's good luck!"

"I am not so sure," Araceli said as she ran to the water's edge. "If that was you, Enrique, that's a rude way to let me know that you are still hanging around! And you have seriously bad aim!"

After washing the poop out of her hair,

Araceli headed back for sun lotion. As she got closer to where her mother was sitting, she saw a large dog grab her beach bag. From where she was standing, Araceli could have sworn the dog was yellowish, like Bartolo.

Her first thought was to scream out 'Bartolo!' Instead, she shouted, "Hey. Stop. That's my beach bag!"

The dog ignored Araceli's cries as he sauntered to the shore, her beach bag in tow. A young man in gray jogging shorts whistled shrilly and loudly yelled, "Tolo! Come here now!"

Before ambling back to its owner, the dog dropped Araceli's beach bag in a sandy puddle near the water's edge.

Could that have been Bartolo?

Araceli sprinted to grab her bag. The dog was about the size of Bartolo. His fur was tangled and yellowish. He also moved in a lumbering kind of way, sort of like Bartolo.

Araceli pulled on the bag's pull strings. The seashell was still in one piece. Again, she wondered; She was sure she had heard the dog's owner call him 'Tolo', which is Bartolo for short.

As Araceli stood at the water's edge, she brooded: *If only Enrique, Paquito, and Bartolo would just show up, talking, flying, hopping just like they had yesterday and the day before. Would they ever show up again?*

A Gift to the Future

Araceli wasn't sure of anything. But the dog had come out-of-the-blue, grabbed her beach bag and set it down at the seashore. That had to mean something! But what?

Araceli trudged back to where her mom was now listening to a battery-operated radio she always brought to the beach. "You can't always get a signal at the beach with the new devices," she explained to Araceli, who thought the radio was ancient and old-fashioned.

Araceli plopped down next to her mom on a blanket they had spread over the sand. "Have you ever thought that someone you just met was really someone you once knew?" she asked.

Her mom responded thoughtfully. "Well, someone can look or act like someone else you might know. So yes.

They can remind you of someone else."

"I don't mean like *that*," said Araceli. " I mean did you think they were the same person, but in another form, even if it was an animal?"

"Well, I guess it all depends on what you believe," her mom said. "Let me tell you a story."

Her mom scooped up some sand and let it dribble through her fingers. Then she began. "One day I went to place some flowers at your abuelo's memorial. I sat on the bench feeling quite sad because I missed him so much. I blurted out, 'Oh, Papá, I wish that I could see you again.' Well, at that moment a dragonfly landed majestically on my knee! It looked beautiful with its blue-green, fluorescent see-through wings. It was so close I could see its round crystal-like eyes staring right into mine! I felt as if the dragonfly had touched my spirit. To this day, anytime I

95

see a dragonfly, I think it's your abuelo's spirit, hitching a ride to say hi!"

Araceli sprung up.

"Would you believe me if I told you that the bird that pooped on my head, and the dog that grabbed my beach bag were trying to tell me something?"

Araceli's mom was about to respond when a frantic voice on the radio grabbed her attention.

"This is breaking news!"

Araceli went on, "I think I know what I need to do now, Mom, I…."

"Hush a minute," said her mom. "There's a hurricane that might come close to the island. Perhaps that's what the news is about."

"Last night," said the voice on the radio, "police departments all over the island were flooded with calls from concerned citizens who reported seeing bright lights in the sky. Here on the island some said the lights were coming from El Yunque National Forest. Many reported hearing loud music, while others swore they saw hot air balloons floating over the ocean. We also got reports from news outlets worldwide about a loud wonk sound, followed by a catchy tune people can't stop humming. Authorities are investigating. The story will be updated as more information becomes available."

Araceli and her mom both stared at the radio, hypnotized by every word.

Music resumed playing on the radio immediately after the announcement.

"You know what," said Araceli's mom. "I think I'm starting to remember some of the lyrics to the tune I was humming this morning: *Do you smile when you hear the* coquí *sing, "Coquí. Coquí,"* hum, hum, hum… *"How do you feel when the gray wolf howls in the moonlight? …*hum, hum, hum."

"I know the whole song," Araceli said quietly as she reached for her mom's hand, and lead her toward the seashore.

Her mom followed without saying a word.

When they reached the seashore, Araceli pulled out the seashell. "This is the seashell that made that wonk sound."

Araceli's mom was silent for a moment. She fixed her gaze at the seashell, then at Araceli, not completely sure of what was happening or what to say. But as she noticed Araceli's serious expression, she said, "What do you think the poopy bird and the dog were trying to tell you?"

"The poopy bird is named Enrique, and the dog is Bartolo," Araceli said. "Have you ever heard of the *Alarma de Caracol?*"

"For the Taino people who lived on this island a long time ago, the *Alarma de Caracol* was used to warn of approaching danger."

Araceli smiled widely and told her mom the story that Paquito had told her about the brave Taino warriors who almost fell out of the canoe, and how the seashell had fallen deep into the sea.

"Would you believe this is the same seashell, and that I blew into it so people could pay more attention to animals that might disappear from the entire planet?"

"You are talking to someone who believes abuelo hitchhikes on the backs of dragonflies," her mom said smiling. At that moment Araceli knew that she could tell her mom anything, including about her trip to El Toro Peak last night. But she didn't, not at that moment.

She turned to her mom and said, "I believe that Bartolo wants me to return the seashell to the sea. We took one small step. We got the world's attention. Someone in the future may need to find the seashell to sound *La Alarma de Caracol* to warn them of something that might need attention."

Araceli started into the water, then looked at her mom.

"I have to walk deeper into the water. That way I can throw the seashell further into the ocean. Is that okay?"

"Be careful, corazón," her mom said. "I'll wait here for you."

Araceli took a small step into the ocean. She kept taking one small step after another, until she was waist deep. She held on tightly to the seashell. When she found a spot where she believed the seashell should lie, she stopped.

Before dropping the seashell into the ocean, she traced the snail etching and smiled as she remembered the pushy snail who had taken her, Paquito, Enrique, and Bartolo to the top of El Toro Peak. Then she peered deep into the seashell to make sure Paquito, who once had crawled into it, was not there now.

Thank goodness that she did!

"We meet again!" exclaimed a cheerful voice.

Araceli nearly dropped the seashell as she recognized Paquito's voice. "I could have dropped you into the ocean!" Araceli yelled.

"But you didn't," Paquito said as he hopped from the seashell to Araceli's shoulders. "Aren't you happy to see me?"

Araceli replied with her own question.

"What are you doing here?"

"Just here to help a friend," he told her. "Together, let's give the future a gift."

"Let's do it," Araceli agreed, suddenly feeling a rush of happiness. "On the count of three, I'm dropping the seashell back into the sea."

Together, Araceli and Paquito counted: "one…two…three!"

Neither of them moved as they watched the magic seashell drift slowly to the bottom of the sea.

"Hang on tight," Araceli said. "I see my mother waving for me to return."

As Araceli waded carefully back to the shore with Paquito on her shoulder, together they sang:

We sing to the stars.
We sing to the trees.
We sing to the wind.
We sing to the stones.
We sing to every blade of grass.
We dearly sing to you.

Listen. Listen.
See us. Hear us. Save us.
We are one.
We are one.

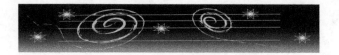

About the Author

The author lives in Buda, Texas with her two cats, Picasso, and El Greco, and with their cat friend, Finn. This is the first book for the author. In the works, however, is a nonfiction book about the Puerto Rican parrot and its' struggle to survive.

The author earned an undergraduate degree from Brandeis University in Waltham, Massachusetts, and a master's degree from the University of Texas at Austin. In her spare time, the author loves to read, paint, and frolick through forests, mountains and beaches everywhere.

Lightning Source UK Ltd.
Milton Keynes UK
UKHW041320050323
418057UK00001B/109

9 798218 113582